CUENTO
DE LUZ

For Danièle and José Manuel, who have cleared the snow
from the tracks of our train so many times.

- Susanna Isern -

For Irene and Rebeca, my traveling companions.

- Ester García -

Text © Susanna Isern
Illustrations © Ester García
This edition © 2014 Cuento de Luz SL
Calle Claveles 10 | Urb Monteclaro | Pozuelo de Alarcón | 28223 | Madrid | Spain
www.cuentodeluz.com
Title in Spanish: Tren de invierno
English translation by Jon Brokenbrow

ISBN: 978-84-15784-84-5

Printed by Shanghai Chenxi Printing Co., Ltd. April 2014, print number 1426-4

FSC
www.fsc.org
MIX
Paper from
responsible sources
FSC® C007923

THE WINTER TRAIN

SUSANNA ISERN   ESTER GARCÍA

Dawn was breaking in the Northern Forest, as the leaves fell from the trees. The animals woke up and started to pack their bags.

"Help! I can't find my toothbrush!" said
Wild Cat worriedly.
   "I need another suitcase. Can anyone
lend me one?" said Deer, who was quite vain.
   "Don't forget to turn off the light, Rabbit.
Last year it was on for more than six months!"
said Badger.

Once their bags were packed, it was time
to say good-bye.

"Don't worry about me," said White Owl.
"Someone's got to stay behind and look
after the forest. Anyway, I love the cold!"

"Winter goes by really fast. We'll be fine!"
said Frog to the fish, who were swimming sadly
in the river.

"I'll miss you, den," said Fox, waving good-bye
to his home.

At midday they all met at the foot of the oldest tree.
That was where the train stopped.

"Every time we leave the Northern Forest,
I feel homesick," sighed Partridge.

"And when we leave the Southern Forest, we feel exactly the same," said Hedgehog. "Hang on! Wait! Don't leave me here!" yelled Tortoise, who was the last to arrive, as usual.

Then suddenly...

Choo choo! Choo choo!

The Winter Train was arriving.

Choo choo! Choo choo!

As it did every year at this time, it would take the animals from the Northern Forest to the Southern Forest, where they could spend the cold months in a warmer climate.

Once they were aboard the train, the animals found their seats.

"I prefer to be by the window. Otherwise I get all queasy," said Groundhog.

"I can trust you, can't I?" said Goat, as he sat down next to Wolf.

"I'll be more comfortable in the coat closet," said Bat, who preferred dark places.

And so the Winter Train chugged toward the south. Although the journey would take a few hours, the animals were all in high spirits, chatting, singing, and playing cards.

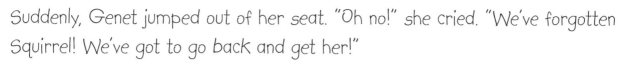

Suddenly, Genet jumped out of her seat. "Oh no!" she cried. "We've forgotten Squirrel! We've got to go back and get her!"

"But if we go back, we could get trapped in the snow," said Beaver, pointing to the dark clouds outside the window.

"We can't leave Squirrel behind. She can't stand the cold," said Ferret.

"Well, that's settled then. Let's go and find her!" said all the animals together.

The conductor brought the train to a halt and turned back.
It got colder and colder, and the first snowflakes began to fall.

When they got back to the Northern Forest, the landscape was covered in a blanket of white. Genet jumped off the train and bounced through the snow toward Squirrel's house.

Squirrel's tree stood in a lonely spot. Genet climbed up the trunk until she reached Squirrel's den. In one corner, her friend was huddled up in a ball. She was shivering so much that Genet could hear her teeth rattling together.

"Squirrel! Come on! The train's waiting for
us!" said Genet, waking her with a start.
    "You came back to rescue me!" said
Squirrel, shuddering from the cold. "Last
night I was counting stars until late, and
when I woke up, the train had already left."

Genet and Squirrel
ran back to the train.
On seeing that Squirrel
was safe, all of the animals
jumped up and down with joy,
and smothered her with hugs and
kisses. The conductor started up the
engine once again, but it had snowed so
much that the train tracks were completely
covered. They were trapped! The sun was setting
behind the mountains, it was getting colder and colder,
and the animals began to lose hope.

After thinking for a while, Bear had a good idea. "Let's try to clear the snow off the tracks. We can do it if we work together."

And so the animals jumped down from the train and began to clear away the snow. Bear shoveled great clumps with his huge claws, while the smallest animals cleaned off the rest with their paws and wings. Soon there was no snow left on the rails.

The heat of the motors had melted the snow closest to the train. Some of the animals also helped by pushing the train from the back.

Then suddenly...

Choo-choo! Choo-choo!

The train started to move.

Choo-choo! Choo-choo!

The animals quickly jumped back onto the train and returned to their seats. They'd done it!

Night fell over the Northern Forest, as the snow covered the trees. Squirrel was still curled up, trying to get warm under Eagle's huge wings. The animals smiled, satisfied. Some of them were holding paws, while others were fast asleep, snoring quietly.

Meanwhile, the Winter Train chugged through the dark, dark night, through the freezing air, toward the promise of the Southern Forest.